Musings Diary

This page is intentionally left blank.

Musings Diary

A Collection

By

HITARTH RAVAL

Copyright Information

This page is intentionally left blank.

Contents

This page is intentionally left blank.

This page is intentionally left blank.

Who are you?

That ever-lasting smile on your face, that undying tenderness in your eyes should never vanish. For that has kept me sated for quite a long time now. You let me forget all those immature tantalizing feelings from the past and make me feel content and tranquil in my life. What should I call you? An angel? Well, I doubt, even an angel could do such things!

Defrost

I was standing in front of you like a senseless sack of goods, virtually making no sane moves – neither physical nor emotional. Then, I realized that I had never been like this in front of anyone. It was your flawless beauty and inexpressible charm that had done the trick and that something mysterious about you wanted me to defrost myself in the eternal seeming ice age and just burst into flames passionately!

Concern

...And fearing your departure from my life wasn't the concern then. The never ending anticipation of someone like you – just as existence, as elegant and as loving as you were, was!

Something PHYSIC-al today…

The moment you feel the need to use force in a relationship; back off a little and think wisely. Since, let it be any relationship, a romantic one or not, you absolutely do not require the force element to start or to keep moving ahead in it. Life is not like newton's first law, rather it's like the third one – true love will always have an equal and opposite reaction towards its origin.

A nightmare or reality?

The irritating sensations in my mind started, when I saw that she was already there. I didn't utter a word and stood near my motel room window. The breeze coming from the window gave me some relief, yet I was in no mood of facing her again. I could see red marks on her neck, but I didn't want to enquire about them. I thought she'd *haunt* me for an hour or two as usual; but to my surprise, she was leaving! Before I could understand anything, she was gone. All I could hear was, 'Please close the door behind me.' I could not understand why she asked me to do that, because the door we used to go through was already closed long ago!

Bound yet Free

It was an interesting journey from the beginning to this day. I don't know where I am today, but I feel safe and cosy here. It took me very long to get to this place and in the meantime, I kept trying to find myself anxiously in all those depths, but all I could find was a reflection, that wasn't even mine, as if something had covered my soul and my body; all I could listen to was my own voice through the same repeating echoes. There was an utter emptiness that had surrounded me then, but I feel FREE now, when I'm finally BOUND to you!

Apprehension

Love isn't feared by hatred. It is stronger than the hate itself. Love is rather feared and diminished because of the *apprehension*. A person, who doesn't know how to swim, fallen into the water doesn't drown solely because of the lack of skills. He drowns because of the apprehension, leading to his death. Similarly, love dies, when you panic too much to lose it!

Powerful weapon

Love is very powerful in itself that it can manipulate all seven basic emotions of a person – anger, fear, joy, sadness, disgust, contempt and surprise. It's therefore, totally upon us how to turn it into our own good.

Final outcome

When love fails, it doesn't necessarily become *hate*. Hate makes a person explode with emotions of outrage, when it goes out of control. A failed love, on the other hand, makes a person implode in himself/herself. Both in their final outcomes are the same though – once it's all over, the person crushes down psychologically!

Harmony

To achieve a state of harmony in (love??) life, one must respect and listen to his/her conscience and act accordingly, because not all the decisions taken by heart will help us in the end.

Retreat

Always retreat and always be ready to explain, even if it is over. For life never gives anyone the chance to get up and give it yet another shot every time!

Incredible creation

You are the peace, the humanity is searching for;

You are the wealth, the poor is seeking for;

You are the light, the *Kaliyuga* is craving for;

For you are still the most incredible creation, the world is demanding for!

Never

True love, unlike dreams, can never be superficial or meaningless.

Trust

Trust has a very crucial value in interpersonal love. Without the trust factor, three out of the six components of love – commitment, intimacy and passion, will fail eventually. Forget about the lust, attraction and attachment. They are long gone – the moment you broke that trust!

Hate

Don't let your hate towards someone overcome your inner self, because when you let the hate build its house in your heart, it eventually becomes either your disposition or your attitude, hurting *you* only.

It's simple!

Admire her way of dressing.

Praise her cookery.

Encourage her interests.

Fulfil her dreams.

Rectify her mistakes.

Share her sorrows.

Protect her body.

Love her inner self.

Give her your time.

That's how you win her! It's simple!

Heartbeats

Lying on a hospital bed in some ICCU; heartbeats being monitored, I wished she would at least come and see me in my last days, after all these years of separation. She did come, indeed, to *visit* me and my heart responded to her presence by skipping a beat… once again!

*The ECG just then showed I'd flat lined.

Emotions are weird

Sometimes it is not the question of who you are to me. Sometimes it might not be the question of what you mean to me. You just need to trust your instincts and follow what your heart says. Because, the people, who you feel, are important to you, don't necessarily feel the same way for you!

Limit

When two persons are in genuine love with each other, and that relationship is not destroying anything else, then it's solely their business. No third person, however close to either or both of them, has the right to invade the privacy or the relationship. It's as simple as that. One has to define a limit here. I don't get why people have such a hard time digesting this. The society is full of people, who are happy interfering and ruining others' businesses, even if they don't have to do so. That is not acceptable.

Break free

What you have felt till now is that you are pretty tough to be understood. You think that people around you generally don't get you and that's why they are unable to love you. You first need to break free of your chains and expect the love from within, because there is probably and there will always be someone who will hold onto you, no matter how you feel about it all. You must expect the love once you are ready to accept it.

Validity

It's dramatic how people shift away from you, when time changes. These were the same people, who were so intimate with you at times that the world thought you were literally inseparable. Suddenly, nothing extraordinary happens and after years, now you see the same people chilling out with others. It's consequential that they make you feel that they are all busy with their lives. You were there with them, too, when someone else would have felt this way. One of my dearest friends had told me once, 'People come in your life with a certain validity period and once the validity expires, you're either all alone or forced to find new ones!' I certainly cannot find a driving force behind this. Can you?

Selfish

It's not about what community we are in or what culture we follow. It's all about us and what kind of a person we want to be with! If we have double standards about certain people, then we will keep changing the definition of the *perfect partner* that we all are looking for. The list of requirements keeps changing forever. We think we just love a person, because he/she is good looking, rich, famous or has a good nature. In fact, at the end, it all comes down to one thing and that is, 'What is our personal benefit from spending our time/life with that person?' We are all selfish, including those who say they are in *unconditional love*.

Black Hole

You cannot expect to put out fire with fire. You are going to need something opposite in nature. You can always keep building your relationship with a like-minded hot head. Result? Similar to what happens to a large star … you would eventually crush under your own load and collapse into a Black hole!

Another world, may be?

I wish there could be another world full of hopeless romantics, because this world is so much extra practical, that no matter how hard I try, I end up being a fool in that system!

What goes around, comes around!

What goes around, comes around, as they say. I cannot help but wonder, why does not this feel true, especially, when it comes to good deeds? Life is a mystery and sometimes it becomes almost impossible to unravel. You get so lost in its maze, that you start to think there is no way out. Nothing makes sense anymore, because the very laws that you were raised to respect have become useless. They protect the evil ones and throw the good ones in gaols. You start to think nothing is worth it anymore. Being good starts to seem like it is overrated. You are good for so long and still, you watch as life passes you by. You fold your hands and remain good despite the fact that the bad and corrupted ones around you make headway, while you seem stuck at one point. You're tempted, highly tempted to just throw those values away and become a predator. You want to hunt mercilessly, until you get what you want. You want to let your inner animal out... Don't do it, the law of *Karma* is real. What goes around really does come around. Never forget that.

Make a choice

You're in love with him. That's what you tell yourself every time he hits you. You look forward to the day when he becomes his sweet self. That was the man you fell in love with and you wait breathlessly for him to come back to you. On the days that he does, you tell yourself that the punches and the blows are all worth it. You believe you will do anything to stay in his good graces. So, you grovel and submit and compromise. You do this over and over again, until you have nothing left to give. He goes into the ring every other time to battle his demons and each time they win, he takes his frustrations out on you. You whisper to yourself every night that he'll change.

He'll go back to being the man you married. But you must know this, he'll never change. You leave to live or stay to die. Make a choice. Make a damn choice.

So tell me Mr.

What happens when you find out that it was not worth it? That none of it was worth it really. What will you do when you realize that, while you slaved away for your corporate masters, your children knew you less and less and your wife fell out of love with you?

What will you do when you walk into your empty house on your marble floors and find that no one is there to welcome you back? No delightful screams of welcome or your wife's delightful smile. Tell me, what will you do?

So tell me Miss

What will you do, when you find that you have worked all your life doing something that did not fulfil you? How will you quench the thirst to chase your passion when your bones are too weak to function?

How do you overcome the emptiness and the sadness that is bound to come when you realize that despite all the money and the accolades you have gathered, you are still as empty as an unfilled barrel?

So tell me Mr and Miss, won't you rather do something differently today?

Beauty

When you realize that beauty is really ephemeral, it is usually too late to do anything about it. You notice the new wrinkle on your forehead one morning and then another line the next week. You see a strand of white hair that was not there yesterday and you smile, a little sadly… Time is catching up to you and the beauty that you once worshipped is disappearing. Then you realize just how true it. The sentence that, 'Beauty is temporary.'

Death

Death comes knocking without warning. Suddenly, in the twinkle of an eye, a body once so filled with life becomes nothing but a pile of flesh. When the reactions start and flesh turns to dust, don't you ever wonder what happens to the man or woman? What happened to the memories and the emotions? The love and the hate they felt when they lived. Don't you ever wonder about these things? Whether or not there is an after-life? Where do the souls go? Is there a rebirth? I wonder about these things a lot. Don't you?

This life of yours

This life of yours is very beautiful; value and cherish it. It is worth more than the gold and diamonds. It remains priceless and you are different, not because you are weird, but because you know who you are, value your existence.

Mentality

These voices we hear all around, give shapes to our mentalities, they give birth to our mentalities; some of these voices are in their lowest tunes and others are in their highest tunes. They all have one thing in common and that is the choice they give us. We can allow them to diffuse into our veins and journey with our blood or we can disallow their entrance like oil does to water. What we allow in, procreate what we will have in.

This heart of ours

We do not change our decisions, because of what others feel about them; we change our minds, because we were not convinced about whatever it was in the first place. This heart of ours is indeed pretty tricky!

Resist a forced change

This world is built upon so many options.

This world is built upon so many decisions.

Don't let anyone force anything on you.

This is your world, don't let anyone rule it for you.

Broken heart

He had just few words to say and a whole lot of tears that had drenched his eye balls. He looked at her and said, 'My words may not be bulky enough, but I do hope my tears speak a thousand words.'

Dreams

I'm often mystified at how hopes and aspirations can be easily discarded, thrown into trash cans and burnt into ashes. If you dream so big, then you should live bigger. If you aim so high you shouldn't be below. If you are below, then you should get yourself up there. Dreams don't become realistic by making them up in our minds nor by writing them down on pieces of papers. Dreams become real when we realize the fact that we are going to do whatever is willing to make them come to reality. Dreams become reality, when we are ready to get them off the surface of our minds and put them into motion. We create the pathways for our dreams to become reality, our dreams don't create pathways for themselves.

Your worth

They might worth more than gold but, diamonds can't raise their standard to your worth.

In the long run

A lot can take place within the span of a year. Love can be found, love can be lost. New friends to journey with, old friends to part with and old perspectives to do away with. The surprising visitation of the new perspectives, that flows through the veins of our bodies because of the experiences we have gone through, because of our hopes and aspirations and because of who we choose to be. So much can take place in a year, that we cannot just imagine what and what not will take place, when we see each other after a long period.

Our words and actions

Those words we say unconsciously go a long way in expressing things we have stored up in our minds. Those actions we perform unconsciously go a long way in defining what we have stored up in our thoughts. We dish them out in our unconscious state of mind.

Hurting heart

Those clenched fist, those red eye balls, those fumes ascending from your head, they all remind me of the man you promised not to be!

Pieces

Maybe if we join your piece of puzzle with mine, we'd make a whole lot of sense!

Drifting heart

Your heart has drifted. Although you claim to be near, you are thousand miles away.

When we love

When we love, we love with all the veins that runs through us. We love with all the blood that flows through us. We love with all our heart. We love with all that we have. We love with all that we hope to be. We love with all the risk embedded in love, knowing fully well that love is not a smooth, but rather a crooked path. When we love, we love with all intensity.

If only

If only he knew.

If only he knew, she didn't need just his wealth.

If only he saw through her.

If only he knew, she wanted more.

If only he had more time to spend with her.

If only he knew she saw through him.

If only he knew she adores who he was than what he had.

If only he understood her depth of thirst for his drifted attention.

If only he knew, then he wouldn't have lost what he had!

Fragments

With every piece of his and every joining, he dreaded who he had become. He had let what he felt toiled with what he knew. He had become a shadow to who he visualized himself to be. He had lost who he was. Now, he has to pick up his fragments and try to fix them together.

Responsibility

That crown on your head shows a lot of responsibility, so be careful how you place it and how you lift it.

In the dark

People attached him to a particular identity, simply because he didn't know what his identity was.

Who they want you to be

People will always try to make you who they want you to be, if you do not know who you are.

Moment

No one knows what the next minute holds and so, I'm going to cherish every minute until there is none left.

Am I?

Am I the only revelation that ends your genesis?

The 'Hellos' that silently turns to 'Goodbyes'

Gently our promises in their so called mighty bonds broke down into mere words. Our long speeches assumed their unusual shortness. These short words grew into *'hi' and 'hellos'*. Our *'hi' and 'hellos'* grew in the light of unconditional silence. You remain my cherished memory, well, not until I text another *'hi'*, and slowly but surely, I will only be able to access the dim memories of us together as they quietly fade away into the bittersweet forgotten world.

We are both puzzle pieces

Do you remember me, when the sun is up and when your arms are up for a stretch? Do you think about me, when your pillow calls for your dear attention at night? Remember the additional happiness that I brought along with the morning sun and the emptiness that I took away during the night time.

Hurt

You didn't break me; neither with your words nor with your actions! I broke myself with the perception of who I thought you would be, the idea of who I expected you to grow to become.

Cold breeze

Much like the cold breeze envelops me, when the heat leaves me with that sudden feeling of shiver.

That's the exact feeling I get, when you are around.

This heart

This heart was made for just one thing. This heart will continue to go on even when you go on with your atrocities. But be sure not to comeback. You've replaced a soft heart with a stony heart!

Love

I'd always love you.

Above every circumstance.

Far beyond any feeling.

I'll build a mansion of trust.

I'll plant a garden of understanding and water it every day.

I'll be by you side, even during the raining days.

Lest I forget, it'd always be between me and a strange man.

But I won't be bothered, because that heart of yours truly longs to be with me.

What breaks us?

We perceive danger from afar, it's not necessarily our way. We put the law into our hands. We remain on the battle field with our feeble hands and hear. We endure the endurable. We feel hurt and broken, forgetting that we choose what to fight. We go on fighting every possible war, even when they are not ours to deal with.

Another image

Chances would have made me prolong the night. I'd have beseeched the day never to come to an end. I wanted to stare at the perfection before me; how incredibly shaped your eyes were, how cutely pointed your nose was. Only one thing held me back and threw me against the wall that it was another image. Not me but someone else. I saw you but you didn't! You see someone else. You pretended I was not a replacement.

We

'We only get to live once', he whispered into my ears. And once we live, we go about through and through; part of us searching for the bright light or for a minute of fame, the other part searched for what completes it.

A broken heart

It's true that I loved you with every breath and every part of me, I saw beyond your flaws and imperfections in a way you made me perfect. My love was not blind nor was it stupid. It was matured and able to look beyond who you were, but, you only loved me with the spaces between your teeth and the tip of your tongue.

If

Peradventure I may walk out of this door.

Be sure of my intentions are not to return at all.

I'll go far away.

Across the seas and oceans.

I'll walk out of your life.

You'd never even have the chances to see my shadow.

When he knows

He sees sincerity, he sees vulnerability, when tears strolls down the path of her face. The levity of her tears were greater than those of her words. He knows the level of sincerity she was trying to pass across.

Peace

I know a place.

Far away from the voices in the wind.

Far away from provoking scenarios.

Far away from lies and deceit.

Far away from all the odds.

Far away from this external pollution.

My place of serenity.

Here in this mind of mine.

I walked away

Fear griped me, disappointment held me down and I wanted to steal another glance. May be this time, I might be able to say my goodbye; may be this time, I might be able to voice out; may be this time, I would be able to give my all and then it dawned on me that instance, 'I can't be held down while she was chasing after someone else.'

Not your kind of air

I always thought I was the oxygen she breathes in, and then I realized I wasn't even anything near to that at all. I was the carbon dioxide, that type she wasn't supposed to breathe in. She was choking and I never took notice until she mumbled, 'You weren't made to complete me'

What she never did

She never completed any statement, and I was at the receiving end. I was never led out of my corner of confusion. With the spaces between her teeth, she would speak empty nothings and I thought to myself the reason she doesn't complete her words would be something else. Could it be that I am not worth the completion?

Warnings

We see through circumstances.

We choke the words flowing out from our hearts.

We make life miserable for those words.

And over time these circumstances turn around, when those words are dead and long gone already.

Then, it hits us that we have killed something.

It hits us that we have forcefully choked a life.

We pretend like it didn't happen and we drain the life of our inner conscience.

Now you see me, later you won't

I endured every breath.

I endured every word.

I endured every action.

I was tagged a super endurance man.

Slowly and gently, my heart became used to those ugly words.

Hearing those words became a living part of me.

'I would survive', I mumbled.

My heart became crestfallen.

My humane became rebellious.

There had been a switch of personality and there I was done enduring and ready to walk out!

Words

I have always built myself up over and over again and unknowingly, I have always given access to the thieves to pull a well concreted block out of my walls. They were images of cyclones and now they wonder how I became deaf. I shut my ears to the voices around me, to the voices humming over me. I was trying to rebuild myself again and this time, I was trying to prevent thieves from pulling down my concreted walls out which was making me feel like I'm incomplete. This time I've decided to be made whole.

Betrayal

She saw through me.

Through my weakness and every flaw.

Through my helpless state she saw.

Through my ignorant being she perceived.

Through my naïve being she plotted an attack.

She belittled me.

Cut me into pieces and that's how

She betrayed me!

Commitments

She knew she had to keep going. These were the exact words she spoke to herself. This world was big enough to house her ideas, big enough to contain them all. She knew where she was coming from and she knew not to stop forwarding her steps. She couldn't go back and so she kept moving and dancing to the rhythms of her commitments.

Love

She was quite quaint on the matters concerning the heart. But there I was, greatly up-to-date. We both came from two different universe. She's from the universe struggling to give life to words of love; instead she scribbled them down and I'm from the universe that dreaded scribbling down; instead I love to put life into words concerning the matters of heart.

Maybe.

Maybe you didn't realize, but I did.

Maybe you were dead to those feelings which were trying to sprout out from you, but I wasn't.

Maybe you felt nothing, but I felt something strong.

Maybe you just didn't realize that I was standing there all along.

I dreaded the thoughts of that.

Blinded.

I was blinded by the talks.

I became blind to my own principles.

You became the center of my attraction.

My never fading sunshine,

My never choking air,

My *thoughts* about why I really existed,

My thought of being made to remake ourselves.

As blinded as I was, so was our love!

Judas.

'Do you really know how much I love you?' I'd always ask her,

'How deep is that love you've got for me?' she would ask.

'Deep enough to drown.' I would reply.

I did love her, even when she didn't realize that I did.

I did stretch out my hands, even when she wasn't ready to receive my help.

I did offer a shoulder for her to cry on in her darkest hour.

I emptied my trust in her safe.

But she would always remain my Judas,

The woman who was, is and would always stab me at any circumstance.

We shut out reasoning.

We both knew we were not doing what was right. But, hey?

What's wrong with that?

We were slowly tripping into our graves.

We were quietly saying our last goodbyes.

We were not conscious.

We were already dead in love, but this was the death of us.

Safe heaven.

Let's take a trip down town.

To a place where the gentle touch of the rain drop against the floor is heard.

To a place where the sun shines and never go dim, just like our love.

To a place peace meets with serenity.

To a place where hope meets with joy.

To a place where we'll live forever young in love and turn deaf ears to what people have to say, because either they love it or not, you'll be my last.

Cold and silent

I held her hands as she quietly shut her eyes.

'Don't do this' I sounded funny, even when I was drenched in pains.

'Take care of you for me, you'd find someone better' she managed to say.

'Why do I have to do that when I can have you?' I muttered.

'You can't have me no more, I'm gone.' she gave a faint smile.

'You can't do this' I said once again.

'I'll always love you, here and our next life, I promise to come back.' she smiled a bit. 'Just for you' she managed to say,

I watched the cold hands of death grab her and envelope her as she quietly shut her eyes.

She was gone, long gone, more than I realized.

She just needed to pass the message across.

Throwing out the bags

I decided long ago to walk away from these pains.

They come, as inanimate as they seem to be.

They come to prick me,

To drain me,

To wear me out,

To pull down by walls,

To tear me apart,

To remind me of who I used to be.

I still remember you though.

But I'm far from regretting that stage ever occurred.

I'm far from regretting your being there.

I'm happy I passed through you.

I'm stronger now because of you.

I know for sure I'll make it through now.

I only kept her

She didn't appease my humane. But still, I kept her.

I kept her because I was bored. I kept her to stay in the game.

Forgetting that I am toiling with her emotions.

She feels that I'll give up the whole world to settle with her.

She feels I would sacrifice even in my inconvenience.

She feels I would always be there for her.

She feels she has a shoulder to lean on.

I could be a terrible fairytale.

I feed her with lies. Our love was high on lies.

I made her believe and thrive in the presence of lies.

I made her believe I was who I was not.

I made her believe that I could do what I could not.

I made her believe all the words that I altered were the truth.

She believed and trusted me.

I was never true to her... And I was assured I'd hurt myself in the process.

THE END

www.ingramcontent.com/pod-product-compliance
Lightning Source LLC
LaVergne TN
LVHW041336200726

843509LV00009B/737